SEA CHANGE

Also by JORIE GRAHAM

SEA CHANGE
POEMS

JORIE
GRAHAM

An Imprint of HarperCollinsPublishers

HarperCollins books may be purchased for educational, business, or sales promotional use. For information, please write: Special Markets Department, HarperCollins Publishers, 10 East 53rd Street, New York, NY 10022.

FIRST EDITION

Book Design by Fearn Cutler de Vicq

Library of Congress Cataloging-in-Publication Data
Graham, Jorie.
Sea change : poems / Jorie Graham.   — 1st ed.
p. cm.
Includes bibliographical references and index.
ISBN 978-0-06-153717-2
I. Title.
PS 3557.R214S43   2008
811'.54—dc22   2007041372

08   09   10   11   12   ID/RRD   10   9   8   7   6   5   4   3   2   1

for PETER

Acknowledgments

Grateful acknowledgment is made to those editors, colleagues, and friends whose belief in this work made it possible.

Poems first appeared in: *The Boston Review, carnet de route, The London Review of Books, The New Yorker, The New York Review of Books, Poetry, The Liberal, The Electronic Poetry Review.*

CONTENTS

I

II

III

SEA CHANGE

I

SEA CHANGE

One day: stronger wind than anyone expected. Stronger than

ever before in the recording

of such. Un-

natural says the news. Also the body says it. Which part of the body—I look

down, can

feel it, yes, don't know

where. Also submerging us,

making of the fields, the trees, a cast of characters in an

unnegotiable

drama, ordained, iron-gloom of low light, everything at once undoing

itself. Also *sustained,* as in a hatred of

a thought, or a vanity that comes upon one out of

nowhere & makes

one feel the mischief in faithfulness to an

idea. Everything unpreventable and excited like

mornings in the unknown future. Who shall repair this now. And how the future

takes shape

too quickly. The permanent is ebbing. Is leaving

nothing in the way of

trails, they are blown over, grasses shoot up, life disturbing life, & it

fussing all over us, like a confinement gone

insane, blurring the feeling of

the state of

being. Which did exist just yesterday, calm and

true. Like the right to

privacy—how strange a feeling, here, the *right*—

consider your affliction says the

wind, do not plead ignorance, & farther and farther
away leaks the

past, much farther than it used to go, beating against the shutters I
have now fastened again, the huge mis-
understanding round me now so
still in

the center of this room, listening—oh,
these are not split decisions, everything
is in agreement, we set out willingly, & also knew to
play by rules, & if I say to you now
let's go

somewhere the thought won't outlast
the minute, here it is now, carrying its North
Atlantic windfall, hissing Consider
the body of the ocean which rises every instant into
me, & its
ancient e-
vaporation, & how it delivers itself

to me, how the world is our law, this indrifting of us
into us, a chorusing in us of elements, & how the
intermingling of us lacks in-
telligence, makes

reverberation, syllables untranscribable, in-clingings, & how wonder is also what
pours from us when, in the
coiling, at the very bottom of
the food
chain, sprung

from undercurrents, warming by 1 degree, the in-
dispensable

plankton is forced north now, & yet farther north,
spawning too late for the cod larvae hatch, such

that the hatch will not survive, nor the
species in the end, in the the right-now forever un-

                         interruptible slowing of the

                         gulf

stream, so that I, speaking in this wind today, out loud in it, to no one, am suddenly

                         aware

                         of having written my poems, I feel it in

                         my useless

hands, palms in my lap, & in my listening, & also the memory of a season *at its*

                         full, into which is spattered like a

                         silly cry this in-

                         cessant leaf-glittering, shadow-mad, all over

                         the lightshafts, the walls, the bent back ranks of trees

                         all stippled with these slivers of

                         light like

breaking grins—infinities of them—wriggling along the walls, over the

                         grasses—mouths

                         reaching into

                         other mouths—sucking out all the

air—huge breaths passing to and fro between the unkind blurrings—& quicken

                         me further says this new wind, &

                         according to thy

                         judgment, &

I am inclining my heart towards the end,

                         I cannot fail, this Saturday, early pm, hurling myself,

wiry furies riding my many backs, against your foundations and your

                         best young

tree, which you have come outside to stake again, & the loose stones in the sill.

EMBODIES

Deep autumn & the mistake occurs, the plum tree blossoms, twelve
                                blossoms on three different
branches, which for us, personally, means none this coming spring or perhaps none on
                                just those branches on which
                                just now
lands, suddenly, a grey-gold migratory bird—still here?—crisping,
                                multiplying the wrong
                                air, shifting branches with small
hops, then stilling—very still—breathing into this oxygen which also pockets my
                                looking hard, just
                                that, takes it in, also my
                                thinking which I try to seal off,
my humanity, I was not a mistake is what my humanity thinks, I cannot
                                go somewhere
else than this body, the afterwards of each of these instants is just
                                another instant, breathe, breathe,
my cells reach out, I multiply on the face of
                                the earth, on the
mud—I can see my prints on the sweet bluish mud—where I was just
                                standing and reaching to see if
those really were blossoms, I thought perhaps paper
                                from wind, & the sadness in
me is that of forced parting, as when I loved a personal
                                love, which now seems unthinkable, & I look at
the gate, how open it is,
                                in it the very fact of God as
invention seems to sit, fast, as in its saddle, so comfortable—& where
                                does the road out of it

go—& are those torn wires hanging from the limbs—& the voice I heard once after I passed
                              what I thought was a sleeping
man, the curse muttered out, & the cage after they have let
                              the creatures
out, they are elsewhere, in one of the other rings, the ring with the empty cage is
                              gleaming, the cage is
to be looked at, grieving, for nothing, your pilgrimage ends here,
                              we are islands, we
                              should beget nothing &
what am I to do with my imagination—& the person in me trembles—& there is still
                              innocence, it is starting up somewhere
even now, and the strange swelling of the so-called Milky Way, and the sound of the
                              wings of the bird as it lifts off
suddenly, & how it is going somewhere precise, & that precision, & how I no longer
                              can say for sure that it
knows nothing, flaming, razory, the feathered serpent I saw as a child, of stone, &
                              how it stares back at me
from the height of its pyramid, & the blood flowing from the sacrifice, & the oracles
                              dragging hooks through the hearts in
                              order to say
what is coming, what is true, & all the blood, millennia, drained to stave off
                              the future, stave off,
& *the armies on the far plains,* the gleam off their armor now in this bird's
                              eye, as it flies towards me
then over, & the sound of the thousands of men assembled at
                              all cost now
the sound of the bird lifting, thick, rustling where it flies over—only see, it is
                              a hawk after all, I had not seen
clearly, it has gone to hunt in the next field, & the chlorophyll is
                              coursing, & the sun is
sucked in, & the chief priest walks away now where what remains of
                              the body is left
as is customary for the local birds.

THIS

Full moon, & the empty tree's branches—correction—the tree's
                                    branches,
expose and recover it, suddenly, letting it drift and rise a bit then
                                    swathing it again,
treating it like it was stuff, no treasure up there growing more
                                    bluish and ablaze,
as the wind trussles the wide tall limbs in-
                                    telligently
in its nervous ceaselessness—of this minute, of that minute—
                                    All the light there is
playing these limbs like strings until
                                    you can
                                    hear the
icy offering of winter which is wind in trees blocking and
                                    revealing moon & it's
cold &
                                    in the house someone is
sending instructions. Someone thinks death can be
                                    fixed.
Inside it is magic, footprints are never made
                                    visible. The moon slicks along this human coming and
going with no prints to it. The moon
                                    all over the
                                    idea that this "all"
could be (and no one would mind) a
                                    game. Noise, priests, provinces, zip codes
coil up out of the grasses

towards it. Groups

seize power. Honor exists. Just punishment exists. The sound of

servants not being

set free. Being told it is postponed again. Hope as it

exists in them

now. Those that were once living how they are not

here in this

moonlight, & how there are things one feels instantly

ashamed about in it, & also, looking at it,

the feeling of a mother tongue in the mouth—& how you can, looking away,

make those trees lean, silvered, against

the idea of the universal—really lean—their tips trying to

scratch at it—

Until it sizzles in one: how one could once give birth, that's what the shine

says, and that distant countries

don't exist, enemies do, and as for the great mantle of

individuality (gleaming) &

innocence & fortune—look up: the torturer yawns waiting for his day to be

done—he leans against

the trees for a rest, the implement shines, he looks up.

GUANTÁNAMO

Waning moon. Rising now. Creak, it goes. Deep

over the exhausted continents. I wonder says my

fullness. Nobody nobody says the room in which I

lie very still in the

darkness watching. Your heart says the moon, waning & rising further. Where is it. Your

keep, your eyes your trigger

finger your spine your reasoning—also better to

refuse touch,

keep distance, let the blood run out of you and the white stars gnaw you, & the thorn

which is so white outside in the field,

& the sand which is sheetening on the long beach, the soldiers readying, the up-glance

swift when the key words, of prayer, before

capture, are

uttered, a shiver which has no hate but is not love, is neutral, yes, un-

blooded, as where for instance a bud near where

a hand is unlocking a

security-catch calls

out, & it is an instance of the nobody-there, & the sound of water darkens, & the wind

moves the grasses, & without

a cry the cold flows like a watchdog's

eyes, the watchdog keeping his eye out for difference—only difference—& acts being

committed in your name, & your captives arriving

at *your* detention center, there, in your

eyes, the lockup, deep in your pupil, the softening-up, you paying all your attention

out, your eyes, your cell, your keep, your hold,

after all it is yours, yes, what you have taken in, grasp it, grasp

this, there is no law, you are not open to

prosecution, look all you'd like, it will squirm for you, there, in this rising light, protected

from consequence, making you a

ghost, without a cry, without a cry the

evening turning to night, words it seemed were everything and then

the legal team will declare them exempt,

exemptions for the lakewater drying, for the murder of the seas, for the slaves in their

waters, not of our species, exemption named

go forth, mix blood, fill your register, take of flesh, set fire, posit equator, conceal

origin, say you are all forgiven, say these are only

counter-resistant coercive interrogation techniques, as in give me your

name, give it, I will take it, I will re-

classify it, I will withhold you from you, just like that, for a little while, it won't hurt

much, think of a garden, take your mind off

things, think sea, wind, thunder, root, think tree that will hold you

up, imagine it holding you

up, choose to be who you are, quick choose it, that will help. The moon is colder

than you think. It is full of nothing like

this stillness of ours. We are trying not to be noticed. We are in stillness as if it were an

other life we could slip into. In our skins

we dazzle with nonexistence. It is a trick of course but sometimes it works. If it

doesn't we will be found, we will be made to

scream and crawl. We will long to be forgiven. It doesn't matter for what, there are no

facts. Moon, who will write

the final poem? Your veil is flying, its uselessness makes us feel there is

still time, it is about two now,

you are asking me to lose myself.

In this overflowing of my eye,

I do.

UNDERWORLD

After great rain. Gradually you are revealing yourself to me. The lesson carves

 a tunnel through

an occupied territory. Great beaches come into existence, are laved for centuries, small

 play where the castles are

built, the water carried up for moats, the buckets lost at the end of the exciting

 day, then even the dunes go under, it takes a long while but then

 they are gone

altogether, ocean takes the place, as today where the overpass revealed the fields gone

 under &, just at the surface of the water, the long

miles of barbed wire, twice-there, the ones below (of water) trembling, the fence-posts'

 small fixed pupils staring up

 every fifty feet

at the sky, glittering, their replicas shivering, the spines of grasses gnawed-at by the sick

 human eye, when will we open them

again our eyes, this must all be from the world of shut eyes, one's temples feel

 the cold, maybe one is

 inside a seashell, one is what

 another force

is hearing—how lovely, we are being handed over to an other force, listen, put

 this to your ear—the last river we know loses its

form, widens, as if a foot were lifted from the dancefloor but not put down again, ever,

 so that it's not a

dance-step, no, more like an amputation where the step just disappears, midair, although

 also the rest of the body is

missing, beware of your past, there is a fiery apple in the orchard, the coal in the under-

 ground is bursting with

 sunlight, inquire no further it says,

it wishes it were a root, a bulb, a closed fist—look how it fills
                          with meaning when
opened—then when extended—let us not
                          go there—broken, broken—no to the imagination of some great
                          murmuring through the soil as through the souls of
                          all men—
silent agreement which is actually the true soil—but there it is now going under—nothing
                          will grow in it—the footsteps are washed away which might have
attempted kindness or cultivation or a walk over the earth to
                          undertake
curiosity—that was our true gift to creation: curiosity—how we would
                          dream eyes closed in fog all through the
storm, then open up to aftermath, run out to see—& then of course too much, too
                          much—too much wanting to know—sorry I did not mean to
                          raise my voice—I will turn
no further—you are making yourself punishable says the flood—I will
                          drink it, I will, my God gave
it me says the evaporation sluicing the invisible surfaces,
                          in which clouds are being
said, right into the shuddering of time, its so-called passing—each land
                          had its time for being
born, each date a cage shrinking—until the creature has ribs that bend-in and a skull that is
                          forced
into its heart, & the rain is falling chattering pearling completely turning-in, turning, lost,
                          & all the words that might have held it, it now
                          flows through,
& the rim of the meaning crumbles—& it is the new world you wanted—& it is beginning
                          its life now.

FUTURES

Midwinter. Dead of. I own you says my mind. Own what, own
                            whom. I look up. Own the looking at us
say the cuttlefish branchings, lichen-black, moist. Also
                            the seeing, which wants to feel more than it sees.
Also, in the glance, the feeling of owning, accordioning out and up,
                            seafanning,
& there is cloud on blue ground up there, & wind which the eye loves so deeply it
                            would spill itself out and liquefy
                            to pay for it—
& the push of owning is thrilling, is spring before it
                            is—is that swelling—is the imagined fragrance as one
bends, before the thing is close enough—wide-
                            eyed leaning—although none of this can make you
                            happy—
because, looking up, the sky makes you hear it, you know why we have come it
                            blues, you know the trouble at the heart, blue, blue, what
pandemonium, blur of spears roots cries leaves master & slave, the crop destroyed,
                            water everywhere not
                            drinkable, & radioactive waste in it, & human bodily
waste, & what,
                            says the eye-thinking heart, is the last color seen, the last word
heard—someone left behind, then no behind—
                            is there a skin of the I own which can be scoured from inside the
                            glance—no,
                            cannot—& always
                            someone walking by whistling a
                            little tune, that's

life he says, smiling, there, that was life—& the heart branches with its
                              wild arteries—I own my self, I own my
leaving—the falcon watching from the tree—I shall torch the crop that no one else
                              have it whispers the air—
& someone's swinging from a rope, his rope—the eye
                              throbbing—day a noose looking for a neck—
the fire spidery but fast—& the idea of
                              friends, what was that, & the day, in winter, your lower back
                              started acting up again, & they pluck out the eyes at the end for
                              food, & don't forget
                              the meeting at 6, your child's teacher
                              wishes to speak to you
about his future, & if there is no food and the rain is everywhere switching-on as expected,
                              & you try to think of music and the blue of Giotto,
& if they have to eat the arms he will feel no pain at least, & there is a
                              sequence in which feeding takes
place—the body is owned by the hungry—one is waiting
                              one's turn—one wants to own one's
                              turn—and standing there,
don't do it now but you might remember kisses—how you kissed his arm in the sun
                              and
                              tasted the sun, & this is your
address now, your home address—& the strings are cut no one
                              looks up any longer
                              —or out—no—&
one day a swan appeared out of nowhere on the drying river,
                              it
was sick, but it floated, and the eye felt the pain of rising to take it in—I own you
                              said the old feeling, I want
                              to begin counting
again, I will count what is mine, it is moving quickly now, I will begin this
                              message "I"—I feel the
smile, put my hand up to be sure, yes on my lips—the yes—I touch it again, I

begin counting, I say *one* to the swan, *one,*

do not be angry with me o my god, I have begun the action of beauty again, on

the burning river I have started the catalogue,

your world,

I your speck tremble remembering money, its dry touch, sweet strange

smell, it's a long time, the smell of it like lily of the valley

sometimes, and pondwater, and how

one could bend down close to it

and drink.

II

LATER IN LIFE

Summer heat, the first early morning

        of it. How it lowers the pitch of the

        cry—human—cast up

as two words by the worker street-level

        positioning the long beam on

the chain as he calls up to the one handling the pulley on

        the seventh floor. One

        call. They hear each other!

Perfectly! As the dry heat, the filled-out leaves, thicken the surround, the warming

        asphalt, & the lull in growth

        occurs, & in it the single birdcries now and again

        are placed, &

all makes a round from which sound is sturdied-up without dissipation or dilation,

        bamboo-crisp, &

        up it goes up like a thing

        tossed without warp of weight or evidence of

        overcome

gravity, as if space were thinned by summer now to a non-interference. Up it goes, the

        cry, all the

        way up, audible and unchanging, so the man need

not even raise his voice to be heard,

        the dry warm air free to let it pass without

        loss of

        any of itself along

        its way…

I step out and suddenly notice this: summer arrives, has arrived, is arriving. Birds grow

        less than leaves although they cheep, dip, arc. A call

across the tall fence from an invisible neighbor to his child is heard

right down to the secret mood in it the child

also hears. One hears in the silence that follows the great

desire for approval

and love

which summer holds aloft, all damp leached from it, like a thing floating out on a frail but

perfect twig-end. Light seeming to darken in it yet

glow. *Please* it says. But not with the eager need of

Spring! Come what may says summer. Smack in the middle I will stand and breathe. The

future is a superfluity I do not

taste, no, there is no numbering

here, it is a gorgeous swelling, no emotion, as in this love is no emotion, no, also no

memory—we have it all, now, & all

there ever was is

us, now, that man holding the beam by the right end and saying go on his

ground from

which the word and the

cantilevered metal

rise, there is no mistake, the right minute falls harmlessly, intimate, overcrowded,

without pro-

venance—perhaps bursting with nostalgia but

ripening so fast without growing at

all, & what

is the structure of freedom but this, & grace, & the politics of time—look south, look

north—yes—east west compile hope synthesize

exceed look look again hold fast attach speculate drift drift recognize forget—terrible

gush—gash—of

form of

outwardness, & it is your right to be so entertained, & if you are starting to

feel it is hunger this

gorgeousness, feel the heat fluctuate & say

my

name is day, of day, in day, I want nothing to

come back, not ever, & these words are mine, there is no angel to

wrestle, there is no inter-

mediary, there is something I must

tell you, you do not need existence, these words, praise be, they can for now be

said. That is summer. Hear them.

JUST BEFORE

At some point in the day, as such, there was a pool. Of
                                        stillness. One bent to brush one's hair, and, lifting
                                        again, there it was, the
opening—one glanced away from a mirror, and there, before one's glance reached the
                                        street, it was, dilation and breath—a name called out
                                        in another's yard—a breeze from
                                        where—the log collapsing inward of a sudden into its
                                        hearth—it burning further, feathery—you hear it but you don't
                                        look up—yet there it
                                        bloomed—an un-
learning—all byway no birthpain—dew—sand falling onto sand—a threat
                                        from which you shall have
                                        no reprieve—then the
reprieve—Some felt it was freedom, or a split-second of unearthliness—but no, it was far from un-
                                        earthly, it was full of
                                        earth, at first casually full, for some millennia, then
desperately full—of earth—of copper mines and thick under-leaf-vein sucking in of
                                        light, and isinglass, and dusty heat—wood-rings
                                        bloating their tree-cells with more
life—and grass and weed and tree intermingling in the
                                        undersoil—& the
                                        earth's whole body round
                                        filled with
                                        uninterrupted continents of
                                        burrowing—& earthwide miles of
                                        tunnelling by the
mole, bark beetle, snail, spider, worm—& ants making their cross-
                                        nationstate cloths of

soil, & planetwide the

chewing of insect upon leaf—fish-mouth on krill,

the spinning of

coral, sponge, cocoon—this is what entered the pool of stopped thought—a chain suspended in

the air of which

one link

for just an instant

turned to thought, then time, then heavy time, then

suddenly

air—a link of air!—& there was no standing army anywhere,

& the sleeping bodies in the doorways in all

the cities of

what was then just

planet earth

were lifted up out of their sleeping

bags, & they walked

away, & the sensation of empire blew off the link

like pollen—just like that—off it went—into thin air—& the athletes running their

games in Delphi entered that zone in the

long oval of the arena where you run in

shadow, where the killer crowd becomes

one sizzling hiss, where,

coming round that curve the slowness

happens, & it all goes

inaudible, & the fatigue the urgent sprint the lust

makes the you

fantastically alone, & the bees thrum the hillsides, & all the blood that has been

wasted—all of it—gathers into deep coherent veins in the

earth

and calls itself

history—& we make it make

sense—

& we are asked to call it

good.

LOAN

Rain. And aftermath. Untouchable. The gutters cough and rage, & listening

without

hearing we flinch, soul grins to rain

though we ourselves don't know that grin—

& oozings down treetrunks, liquefying,

as if the flanks were clay—& also smoke when rain lets up,

sudden-heat steam, dif-

ferential, sound of churchbells coming out of

nowhere, I hate you someone cries out where the door has slammed, smell of the

light where it pools on sidewalks, smell of

soil, of the five-century oak emptying suddenly, curbspill, fly-off of

small

cheeping birds—so what are we doing says the path,

&, we want to know where everything's

going, runnelling, & what's

really dead here and what's only changing, really, lift

up the stone, pull back the leaves, loam, sod, dirt, ah

so wet, wait till it dries a bit, evaporation and the wings of it slapping about—

all this *taking* which is not *our* taking—

puddles &

how I go to them, to make them trouble me—

water holding sky and time—

cracks in the asphalt where there is

leak, where air is forced out, goes

to, flows down, follows cracks, makes cracks—the

shine

up here all leafdrip, blossomdrip, chain-

link's minuscule cascading from wisteria cup to cup to
soil where the water's just for a moment
milky, bony, but no
it is just water, do you remember it, the faucet flared like a glare of
open speech, a cry, you could say what you
pleased, you could turn it
off, then on again—at will—and how it fell, teeming, too much, all over your
hands, much as you please—from where you are now
try to
feel it—what
was it this thick/thin blurry coil
flowing into the sink, while someone next to you, washing,
recommended rerouting
the bloodflow round the heart, the surgeon a good one, &
we considered the
odds, how the body was always changing under the stress, & get outdoors he said,
take up some golf, might help with sundays
anyway, & all the while
the water running over our clean hands, like that, in front of the mirror, still alive,
someone who had been getting pretty good at
his job—lifeblood—as in grammar
gliding along in its sentence but still grammar—
such must be our reward was what we never thought then,
& through the intersection the extra, the smell of loam, its
overfullness—unable to take any more in—yet feasting—& all of it going nowhere—&
jump in the shower—just like that—
unearth yourself, god-on-us—whose passion was—nothing—no—
that was the
point—no—
it is given—
as in the richness of a rich man, & succulence holding its waters in tight, &
mirage where there is desperate thirst, &
salt, & the day which comes when there are to be no more harvests from now on,

irrigation returns only as history, a thing made of text,

& yet, listen,

there was

rain, then the swift interval before evaporation, & the stillness

of brimming, & the

wet rainbowing where oil from exhaust picks up light, sheds glow, then

echoes in the drains where

deep inside the

drops fall individually, plink,

& the places where birds

interject, & the coming-on of heat, & the girl looking sideways carrying the large

bouquet of blue hydrangeas, shaking the water off, &

the wondering if this is it, or are we in for another round, a glance up, a quick step

over the puddle

carrying speedy clouds,

birdcall now confident again, heat drying, suddenly no evidence of its having been wet—but no, you

didn't even notice it—it rained.

SUMMER SOLSTICE

Here it is now, emergent, as if an eagerness, a desire to say there this is

             done this is

             concluded I have given all I have the store

             is full the

             crop is

in the counsel has decided the head and shoulders of the invisible have been re-

             configured sewn back together melded—the extra

             seconds of light like

hearing steps come running towards me, then here you

             are, you came all this

             distance,

you could call it matrimony it is not an illusion it can be calculated to the last position,

             consider no further think no longer all

             art of

persuasion ends here, the head has been put back on the body, it stands before us

             entire—it has been proven—all the pieces have

been found—the broken thing for an instant entire—oh strange

             addition and sum, here is no other further step

to be taken, we have arrived, all the rest now a falling

             back—but not yet not now now is all now and

here—the end of the day will not end—will stay with us

             this fraction longer—

             the hands of it all extending—

             & where they would have turned away they wait,

there is nothing for now after this we shall wait,

             shall wait that it reach us, this inch of finishing,

in what do you believe it leans out to suggest, slant,

as if to mend it the rip, the longest day of this one year,

not early and not late, un-

earned, unearnable—accruing to nothing, also to no one—how many more will I

see—no—wrong question—old question—how

strange that it be in

truth not now

conceivable, not as a thing-as-such, the personal death of

an I—& the extra millisecond adds itself to this day,

& learns, it too, to interline the cheek of light

given to the widening face

that stares at us holds us excels at

being—stands, dwells, purrs, allows—what can we say to it—standing in it—

quickly it arrives at full, no, not quickly, it

arrives, at fullest, then there it is, the

brim, where the fullness

stocks, pools, feeds, in-

dwells, is a

yes, I look up, I see your face through the window looking up,

see you bend to the

horizon-line,

do not myself look out at it, no, look at you,

at the long life of having-looked as a way of believing

now in your

thinking

face, & how natural the passage of time, and death, had felt to us, & how you

cannot

comprehend the thing you are meant

to be looking

for

now, & you are weighing something, you are out under the sky

trying to feel

the

future, there it is now in your almost invisible

squinting to the visible, & how I feel your heart beat slowly out there in the garden

        as we both see the

        dove

        in the

        youngest acacia,

& how it is making its nest again this year, how it chose the second ranking

        offshoot

again, how the young tree strains at the stake in the wind, & within,

        the still head of the mother sitting as if all time

        came down to

        this, the ringed neck, the

        mate's call from the

roof, & how we both know not to move—me inside at the window, deep summer, dusk,

        you in the line of sight of the

        bird, & also

        of the hawk changing sides of the field as

        usual,

& the swallows riding the lowest currents, reddish, seeking their feed.

FULL FATHOM

& sea swell, hiss of incomprehensible flat: distance: blue long-fingered ocean and its
                         nothing else: nothing in the above visible except
                         water: water and
always the white self-destroying bloom of wavebreak &, upclose
                         roil, &
                         here, on what's left of land,
ticking of stays against empty flagpoles, low tide, free day, nothing
                         being
                         memorialized here today—memories float, yes,
over the place but not memories any of us now among the living
                         possess—open your
hands—let go the scrap metal with the laughter—let go the
                         upstairs neighbor you did not
                         protect—they took him
                         away—let go how frightened you knew he was all
along while you went on with your
                         day—your day overflowing with time and
place—they came and got him—there are manners for every kind of
                         event—he stopped reading and looked up
                         when they came in—didn't anyone tell you
you would never feel at home—that there is a form of slavery in everything—and when was it
                         in your admittedly short
                         life you
were permitted to believe that this lasted
                         forever—remove your hands
from your pockets—take out that laundry list, that receipt for
                         everything you

pawned last night—decide whom to blame—

stick to your

story—exclude expectation of heavenly

reward—exclude

the milk of

human kindness—poisoned from the start—yes—who ever expected *that*

to be the mistake—with all the murderers and miracle workers—the hovering

spidery

fairy tales—kites, angels, missiles, yellow

stars—clouds—those were houses that are his eyes—those were lives that

are his

eyes—those are families, those are privacies, those are details—those are reparation

agreements, summary

judgments, those are multiplications

on the face of the earth that are—those are the forests, the coal seams, the

carbon sinks that are his—

as they turn into carbon sources—his—

and the festering wounds that are—and the granary that burned—and the quick blow

administered to make it

painless, so-

called—his eyes his yes his blows his seed's first

insertion into this our only soil—

& the flower, the cut

flower in my

bouquet here

made this morning from the walk we took, aimless, as if free,

where you asked me to

marry you, & the loaf of

barley, millet and wheat I was able,

as a matter of course, to bring to the table, fresh-

baked,

in life.

THE VIOLINIST AT THE WINDOW, 1918

(after Matisse)

Here he is again, so thin, unbent, one would say captive—did winter ever leave—no one
has climbed the hill north of town in longer than one can remember—something hasn't
been fully loaded—life is blameless—he is a stem—& what here is cyclic, we would so

        need to know

        about now—& if there is

        a top to this—a summit, the highest note, a

        destination—

here he is now, again, standing at the window, ready to

        look out if asked to

        by his

        time,

        ready to take up again if he

        must, here where the war to end all wars has come

        to an end—for a while—to take up whatever it is

        the spirit

must take up, & what is the melody of

        that, the sustained one note of obligatory

        hope, taken in, like a virus,

        before the body grows accustomed to it and it

        becomes

        natural again—yes breathe it in,

        the interlude,

        the lull in the

        killing—up

        the heart is asked to go, up—

open these heavy shutters now, the hidden order of a belief system

        trickles to the fore,

        it insists you draw closer to

the railing—lean out—
time stands out there as if mature, blooming, big as day—& is this not an emaciated
sky, & how
thin is this
sensation of time, do you
not feel it, the no in the heart—no, do not make me believe
again, too much has died, do not make me open this
all up
again—crouching in
shadow, my head totally
empty—you can see
the whole sky pass through this head of mine, the mind is hatched and scored by clouds
and weather—what is weather—when it's
all gone we'll
buy more,
heaven conserve us is the song, & lakes full of leaping
fish, & ages that shall not end, dew-drenched, sun-
drenched, price-
less—leave us alone, loose and undone, everything
and nothing slipping through—no, I cannot be reached, I cannot be duped again says
my head standing now in the
opened-up window, while history starts up again, &
is that flute music in the
distance, is that an answering machine—call and response—& is that ringing in my ears
the furrows of earth
full of men and their parts, & blood as it sinks into
loam, into the page of statistics, & the streets out there, shall we really
be made to lay them out again, & my plagiarized
humanity, whom
shall I now imitate to re-
become
before the next catastrophe—the law of falling bodies applies but we shall not use
it—the law of lateness—

even our loved ones don't know if we're living—

                    but I pick it up again, the

                    violin, it is

                    still here

in my left hand, it has been tied to me all this long time—I shall hold it, my

                    one burden, I shall hear the difference between up

                    and

                    down, & up we shall bring the bow now up &

                    down, & find

the note, sustained, fixed, this is what hope forced upon oneself by one's self sounds

                    like—this high note trembling—it is a

                    good sound, it is an

ugly sound, my hand is doing this, my mind cannot

                    open—cloud against sky, the freeing of my self

from myself, the note is that, I am standing in

                    my window, my species is ill, the

end of the world can be imagined, minutes run away like the pattering of feet in summer

                    down the long hall then out—oh be happy, &

clouds roil, & they hide the slaughterhouse, they loft as if this were

                    not

perpetual exile—we go closer—the hands at the end of this body

                    feel in their palms

                    the great

                    desire—look—the instrument is raised—

& this will be a time again in which to *make*—a time of use-

                    lessness—the imagined human

paradise.

III

NEARING DAWN

Sunbreak. The sky opens its magazine. If you look hard

it is a process of falling

and squinting—& you are in-

terrupted again and again by change, & crouchings out there

where you are told each second you

are only visiting, & the secret

whitening adds up to no

meaning, no, not for you, wherever the loosening muscle of the night

startles-open the hundreds of

thousands of voice-boxes, into which

your listening moves like an aging dancer still trying to glide—there is time for

everything, everything, is there not—

though the balance is

difficult, is coming un-

done, & something strays farther from love than we ever imagined, from the long and

orderly sentence which was a life to us, the dry

leaves on

the fields

through which the new shoots glow

now also glowing, wet curled tips pointing in any

direction—

as if the idea of a right one were a terrible forgetting—as one feels upon

waking—when the dream is cutting loose, is going

back in the other

direction, deep inside, behind, no, just back—&

one is left looking out—& it is

breaking open further—what are you to do—how let it fully in—the wideness of it is staggering—you have to have more arms eyes a

thing deeper than laughter furrows more

capacious than hate forgiveness remembrance forgetfulness history silence

precision miracle—more

furrows are needed the field

cannot be crossed this way the

wide shine coming towards you standing in

the open window now, a dam breaking, reeking rich with the end of

winter, fantastic weight of loam coming into the

soul, the door behind you

shut, the

great sands behind there, the pharaohs, the millennia of carefully prepared and buried

bodies, the ceremony and the weeping for them, all

back there, lamentations, libations, earth full of bodies everywhere, our bodies,

some still full of incense, & the sweet burnt

offerings, & the still-rising festival out-cryings—& we will

inherit

from it all

nothing—& our ships will still go,

after the ritual killing to make the wind listen,

out to sea as if they were going to a new place,

forgetting they must come home yet again ashamed

no matter where they have been—& always the new brides setting forth—

& always these ancient veils of theirs falling from the sky

all over us,

& my arms rising from my sides now as if in dictation, & them opening out from me,

& me now smelling the ravens the blackbirds the small heat of the rot in this largest

cage—bars of light crisping its boundaries—

& look

there is no cover, you cannot reach

it, ever, nor the scent of last night's rain, nor the chainsaw raised to take the first of the

far trees

down, nor the creek's tongued surface, nor the minnow

turned by the bottom of the current—here

is an arm outstretched, then here

is rightful day and the arm still there, outstretched, at the edge of a world—tyrants

imagined by the bearer of the arm, winds listened for,

corpses easily placed anywhere the

mind wishes—inbox, outbox—machines

that do not tire in the

distance—barbed wire taking daysheen on—marking the end of the field—the barbs like a

lineup drinking itself

crazy—the wire

where it is turned round the post standing in for

mental distress—the posts as they start down the next field sorting his from

mine, his from the

other's—until you know, following,

following, all the way to the edge and then turning again, then again, to the

far fields, to the

height of the light—you know

you have no destiny, no, you have a wild unstoppable

rumor for a soul, you

look all the way to the end of

your gaze, why did you marry, why did you stop to listen,

where are your fingerprints, the mud out there hurrying to

the white wood gate, its ruts, the ants in it, your

imagination of your naked foot placed

there, the thought that in that there

is all you have & that you have

no rightful way

to live—

DAY OFF

from the cadaver beginning to show through the skin of the day. The future without

days. Without days of it?

in it? I try to—just for a second—feel

that shape. What weeds-up out of nowhere as you look away for

good. So that you have to imagine

whatever's growing there growing forever. You shall not be back to look

again. The last glance like a footprint before the

thing it was

takes flight. Disturbing nothing, though,

as it is

nothing. Air moving aside air. That breeze. How is this possible, yet it

must be. Otherwise it cannot be said that this

existed. Or that we did, today. Always breathing-in this pre-life, exhaling this post.

Something goes away, something comes

back. But through you. Leaving no trail but self. As trails go not much of

one. But patiently

you travel it. Your self. You hardly disturb anything actually, isn't it strange. For all

the fuss of *being* how little

you disturb. Also like

a seam, this trail. Something is being

repaired. No? Yes. Push *save*. Write your name again to register. It is some

bride, this flesh barely hanging

on, of minutes, of minutiae, of whatever it is

raising now

up through day's skin as a glance, a toss of hand, in con-

versation, as, growing in-

creasingly unburied now, one can begin to see

the speechless toil, there under day's department, under the texture of

keeping-on-
doing-it, whatever it is that has variation in it, that swallows clip, that the
                              trellis of minutes holds letting clouds slip
                              through if you
                              look up—it seems we are
fresh out of ideas—the pre-war life disappeared, just like that, don't look back you'll
                              get stiff-necked—there is exhaust in the air in its
place—the wilderness (try to think of it) does nothing but point to here, how we
                              got here, says it can't stay
                              a minute longer
                              but that we
                              will have to—& day
something I am feeling lean on my shoulders now, & how
                              free it is, this day, how it seems to bend its
                              long neck
over me and try to peer at me, right here, right into my face—how it is so worried in
                              its hollowing-out over me—night in it starting to
trickle down, & the sensation of punishment though still far away, horns in the
                              distance, & how this was a schooling, & plain
truths which shine out like night-bugs in evening, no one can catch them as
                              they blink
                              and waft, & that summer will be here
soon, which is normal, which we notice is normal, & will our fear matter to
                              anything is a thing we
                              wonder, & before you know it
we are ready to begin thinking about something else,
                              while behind us it is approaching at
                              last the day of
days, where all you have named is finally shunted aside, the whole material man-
                              ifestation of so-called definitions, imagine
that, the path of least resistance wherein I grab onto the immaterial and christen it
                              thus and thus &
something over our shoulders says it is good, yes, go on, go on, and we did.

POSITIVE FEEDBACK LOOP

(*June 2007*)

I am listening in this silence that precedes. Forget
                        everything, start listening. Tipping point, flash
                        point,
convective chimneys in the seas bounded by Greenland. Once there was thunder and also
                        salvos at the four corners of the horizon, that was
                        war.
In Hell they empty your hands of sand, they tell you to refill them with dust and try
                        to hold in mind the North Atlantic Deep Water
                        which also contains
contributions from the Labrador Sea and entrainment of other water masses, try to hold a
                        complete collapse, in the North Atlantic Drift, in the
                        thermohaline circulation, this
                        will happen,
fish are starving to death in the Great Barrier Reef, the new Age of Extinctions is
                        now
                        says the silence-that-precedes—you know not what
                        you
are entering, a time
                        beyond belief. Who is one when one calls oneself
                        one? An orchestra dies down. We have other plans
                        for your summer is the tune. Also your
winter. Maybe the locks at Isigny
                        will hold, I will go look at
                        them
tomorrow. I will learn everything there is of this my spouse the future, here in my
                        earth my parents' house, the garden of
                        the continuing to think

about them, there is nothing else *in fact* but the

        past, count the days count the cities you

        have

visited, also what comes to keep you awake, also dew while you finally sleep—can you ever

        enter the strange thing, the name that is yours, that

        "is" you—

the place where the dead put their arms around you, & you can just taste it the

        bitterness, & you would speak for your kind but

they will laugh at you—both the naming and the kind—also thin air will laugh that's what

        it's doing look—

        feather, invisible bog,

positive feedback loops—& the chimneys again, & how it is the ray of sun is taken in

        in freedom, & was there another way for

        this host

        our guest,

we who began as hands, magic of fingers, laying our thresholds stone upon stone,

        stretched skins between life and death,

always smoke rising to propitiate the star that might turn black, quick give back to it

        before it kills you, speed your thought to it,

        till your feet themselves are

        weary not just your

        heart—the

skins, the flesh, the heat, the soil, the grain, the sound of each birdcall heard over the

millennia, autumn's maneuverings into winter, splinters of dream-filled times, beauty

        that pierces, yes, always we were

        vulnerable to

        beauty, why should it be

otherwise—time and its wonders as it passes and things grow, & the rippings of death

        heal, & the blossoms come which one can

        just for a

        minute longer

        look at, take in, & the mind

finds itself uncertain again, it calls, something hangs up on it, just like that, you hear the receiver go down, power and its end,

something else smiling elsewhere on another world,

us in The Great Dying again, the time in which life on earth is all but wiped out

again—we must be patient—we must wait—it is a

lovely evening, a bit of food a bit of drink—we

shall walk

out onto the porch and the evening shall come on around us, unconcealed,

blinking, abundant, as if catching sight of us,

everything in and out under the eaves, even the grass seeming to push up into this our

world as if out of

homesickness for it,

gleaming.

BELIEF SYSTEM

As a species

        we dreamed. We used to

dream. We did not know for sure about

        the other species. By *the mind* we meant

the human mind. Open and oozing with

        inwardness. Thinking was the habitation of a

trembling colony, a fairy tale—of waiting, love—of

        the capacity for

        postponement—we shall put that

        off the majesty of the mind

        said, in the newspapers, walking among the blessed,

        out in the only

lifetime anyone had—in that space—then in the space

        of what one meant by one's

        offspring's

space. The future. How could it be performed by the mind became the

        question—how, this sensation called tomorrow and

        tomorrow? Did you look down at

        your hands just now? The dead gods

        are still being

        killed. They don't appear in

        "appearance." They turn the page for

        us. The score does not acknowledge

        the turner of

        pages. And always the

absent thing, there, up ahead, like a highway ripped open and left hanging in the

        void—only listen—there is no void, no, it is still

material, which is most terrifying, is still expanse, only without you in it, or anything else

in it—the last word you said before

you screamed

still on your tongue, like a taste, your broad warm tongue out of which existence as we

know it was

made. The waves hit the rocks. The sensation of duty dissolves. The rule of

order—of love—of

what? Don't look at me now I'm not

ready. It's a sur-

prise, I want you to be

surprised. The heartbeat on its little wheels. Your given days its chariot. The rendez-

vous awaiting. Nothing

to be done about

that! Also

the poking about in the ashes which was human

curiosity—always the shadow of what the *yes*

which springs from a mind

sparks—of what filled the mind when the *yes* was

felt—also human the

ownership of such

sad hands,

now still slicing everything, so carefully—the lemon is opening, the letter, the glance, the

century, the sky, the forest—oh—the monster, the

valley and the next-on

valley, also the

army, look, what an idea, an army—the long-gone stars making their zodiac—the severed

fingers and the dirt they're tossed onto,

the moon, sliced, the forum, sliced—still those few pillars and the written voice—here it

comes now the jesus, the body full of its organs,

the parts of the stoning, each part—bone, sinew—

each stone—till she's

gone, she's clothes on the

ground with brothers and uncles around—& the space where the blood flows sliced open

there—& the circle of god, the circle of justice—the red eye at the center, the crowd dispersing,

& the halo of arms still hovering

where each

let fly its stone.

ROOT END

The desire to imagine

         the future.

         Walking in the dark through a house you know by

heart. Calm. Knowing no one will be

         out there.

         Amazing

         how you can move among

         the underworld's

         furniture—

the walls glide by, the desks, here a mirror sends back an almost unseeable

         blink—a faraway lighthouse,

         moonlessness—a planet going

         out—here a

knotting of yet greater dark suggests

         a door—a hollow feeling is a stair—the difference between

         up and down a differential—so slight—of

         temperature

         and shift of provenance of

         void—the side of your face

reads it—as if one could almost overhear laughter "down" there, birdcall "up" there—

         although this is only an

         analogy for different

         silences—oh—

         the mind knows our place so

deeply well—you could run through it—without fear—even in this total dark—this is what

         the mind says in you: accelerate!—it is your

         place, you belong, you know it by

heart, place—

not imaginable, nor under-

stood, where death is still an in-

dividual thing, & in the dark outside only the garden, & in each plant at core a thing

by

heart, & *after all these years* the heart says to itself each

beat, & look, if you make yourself think of it,

the roads out there will branch and branch then

vanish,

fanning out, flat, thinning away like root-ends, everywhere going only forward—&

so far from any so-called

city on the

hill, this city of dis-

appearance, root-ends then nothing, thinnest trailings of

all, forgiveness says the dark, smell

me breathe me in I am your inheritance forgive it,

dusk is already crushed tight and cannot be looked into

anymore, the glance between hunter and prey is choked off, under the big tent the

numbered rows grew

numberless long

ago, admittance is

free, as in you have

no choice, we are trying to block out the sound of drums in the distance, blessed be his

name says someone far in front at the

mike, & seats numbered 1 through 6 billion are

reserved, &

the story of the parted lovers, the one from the prior order,

will begin soon, you will see through the dark to it as it will

light itself

of its own accord,

also moonlight, what can filter through of it—&

look hard for where they rise and act, look hard to see

what action was—fine strength—it turns one inside out—

what is this growing inside of me, using me—such that the

wind can no longer blow through me—such that the dream in me grows cellular, then

muscular, my eyes red, my birth a thing I convey

beautifully

down this spiral staircase

made of words, made of

nothing but words—

UNDATED LULLABY

I go out and there she is still of course sitting on the nest, dead-center in-
                                        visible in our flowing big-
                        headed
still young and staked acacia, crown an almost
                                        perfect
                                        circle, dark greens blurring now
in this high wind, wrestling it, compliant too—billion-mouthed transformer of
                                        sun and the carbon molecule—
                                        & you have to stand still and
                                        look in to see her,
there where the wind splits open the head, slashes the branches, & you see her,
                                        & her head does not even turn or
                                        tuck—
heart, jewel, bloom, star—not on any rung as we are on rungs—I can't help but
                                        look,
                                        wind-slicings keep
                                        revealing her, felt-still, absorbent of
light, sound, gaze, idea—I have seen everything bought and sold I think—
                                        the human heart is a
                                        refugee—is standing here always in
                                        its open
                                        market, shouting out prices, in-
audible prices, & wares keep on arriving, & the voices get higher—
                                        what are you worth the map of the world is
shrieking, any moment of you, what is it
                                        worth, time breaks over you and you
                                        remain, more of you, more of you,

asking your questions, ravishing the visible with your inquiry, and hungry, why are you

so hungry, you have already been

fed, close your

mouth, close your neck, close your hands chest mind, close them—& your eyes,

close them—make arrangements to hold

yourself together, that will be needed, make of your

compassion a

crisper instrument, you will need its blade, you will need

bitterness, stand here all you like looking in, you

will need to learn

to live in this prison

of blood and breath,

& the breeze passes by so generously, & the air

has the whole earth in its mind and it thinks it, thinks it, & in the corner of your cell

look carefully, you are of the ones who worship

cruelty—looking in to her nest, the bloom which is your heart opens with

kindness,

you can feel it flow through you as your eyes take her

in—strange sweetness this—high note—held—

but it is in your hands you must look

for the feeling of what is human,

and in your palms feel

what the tall clouds on the horizon oar-in to you—what will forever replace

stillness of mind—

look out for them their armada is not aware of your air-conditioned

office—swimmingly the thunderheads arrive &

when

is the last time you cried out loud, & who are those there

still shuffling through their files,

trying to card-out what to shred

in time, &

are you still giving out character references, to

whom, & the tickets, who paid for them this

time—your

voice, was it raised too high for the

circumstance—were you too

visible,

did you make sufficient progress, is the address still in your pocket, who paid, who left

the tip, the garden, the

love, the thirst—oh who

was so hungry they ate of the heaven, they ate the piece of it, they ripped its

seam—look the stitching is coming

undone—moon, river-in-the-

distance, stars above the tree, wind dying down—why are you

still here—the end of evening has *come*

and gone—crammed to its full with the whole garden and its creatures—why

are you still here, your eyes like mouths—shut them now—&

tuck in your pleasure, tuck it in,

move on into the deeper water, your kind

await you, sprawling in their camps,

longing to be recognized,

& the harsh priest the cold does his nightly round,

& the huge flower of reason blooms, blooms,

& somebody has a newspaper, not today's, no, but some day's,

and if you can find a corner,

you can pick it up—ignoring the squint-eyed girl, the sensation of

falling, the general theory of

relativity, the nest of

meaning—you can sit in your exile

and, to the tune of the latest song, the recording of what was at some moment the song

of the moment, the *it* song, the thing

you couldn't

miss—it was everywhere—everyone was singing it—you can find your

mind

and in the firelight

catch up on that distant moment's news.

NO LONG WAY ROUND

Evening. Not quite. High winds again.

                I have time, my time, as you also do, there, feel

                it. And a heart, my heart, as you do,

remember it. Also am sure of some things, there are errands, this was a voyage, one

                has an ordained part to play....This will turn out to be

                not true

but is operative here for me this evening as the dusk settles. One has to believe

                furthermore in the voyage of others. The dark

                gathers. It is advancing but there is no

progress. It is advancing with its bellyful of minutes. It seems to chew as it

                darkens. There was, in such a time, in addition,

an obligation to what we called telling

                the truth. We

                liked

                the feeling

                of it—truth—whatever we meant by it—I can still

feel it in my gaze, tonight, long after it is gone, that finding of all the fine discriminations,

                the edges, purse holding the goods, snap shut, there,

you got it, there, it is yours it is true—hold onto it as

                light thins

                holding the lavender in its heart, firm, slow, beginning to

hide it, to steal it, to pretend it never had

                existence. At the window, I stand spell-

bound. Your excellency the evening, I begin. What is this trickiness. I am passing

                through your checkpoint to a nation that is

disappearing, is disappearance. My high-ceilinged room (I look

                up) is only going to survive

invisibility

for the while longer we

have the means

to keep it. I look at the pools of light in it. The carpet shining-up its weave—

burgundy, gold, aqua, black. It is an emergency actually, this waking and doing and

cleaning-up afterwards, & then sleep again, & then up you go, the whole 15,000 years of

the inter-

glacial period, & the orders & the getting done &

the getting back in time & the turning it back on, & did you remember, did you pass, did

you lose the address again, didn't the machine spit it up, did you follow the machine—

yes, yes, did, & the

wall behind it

pronounced the large bush then took it

back. I can almost summon it. Like changing a tense. I peer back through this time to

that one. You will not believe it

when the time

comes. Also how we mourned our dead—had

ample earth, took time, opened it, closed

it—"our earth, our

dead" we called

them, & lived

bereavement, & had strict understandings of defeat and victory....Evening,

what are the betrayals that are left,

and whose? I ask now

as the sensation of what is coming places its shoulders on the whole horizon, I see it

though it is headless, intent

fuzzy, possible outcomes

unimaginable. You have your imagination, says the evening. It is all you have

left, but its neck is open, the throat is

cut, you have not forgotten how to sing, or to want

to sing. It is

strange but you still

need to tell

your story—how you met, the coat one wore, the shadow of which war, and how it lifted,

and how peace began again

for that part of

the planet, & the first Spring after your war, & how "life" began again, what

normal was—thousands of times

you want to say this—normal—holding another's

hand—& the poplars when you saw how much they had grown while you were

away—

the height of them! & the paper lantern you were

given to hold—the lightness of it, of its

fire, how it lit the room—it was your room—you were alone in it and free to sleep

without worry and to

dream—winter outside and the embroidered tablecloth—fruit and water—you didn't
even wonder where was the tree that gave such fruit, you lay in blankets as if they were
non-existent, heat was a given, the rain coming down hard now, what a nice sound—you
could ruminate, the mind traveled back in those days, at ease, it recalled the evening's
con-

versation, the light that fell on x's face, how he
turned when a certain person entered the room—you saw him turn—saw shyness then
jealousy enter his eyes as he looked away—and did he see you see him—and the em-
broidered linen handkerchief you saw a frightened woman in the subway slide from her
pocket, use and replace—then sleep was near—somewhere you were a child and then this
now, nightfall and ease, hospitality—

there are sounds the planet will always make, even
if there is no one to hear them.

About the Author

Jorie Graham is the author of eleven collections of poetry, including *The Dream of the Unified Field: Selected Poems 1974-1994*, which won the Pulitzer Prize. She divides her time between western France and Cambridge, Massachusetts, and teaches at Harvard University.